THE MAGIC FINGER

On the ground below the Greggs stood the four enormous ducks, as tall as men, and three of them were holding guns in their hands. One had Mr. Gregg's gun, one had Philip's gun, and one had William's gun.

The guns were all pointing right up at the nest.

"No! No! No!" called Mr. and Mrs. Gregg both together. "Don't shoot! Please don't shoot!"

"Why not?" said one of the ducks. "You are always shooting at us."

"Oh, but that's not the same!" said Mr. Gregg. "We are *allowed* to shoot ducks."

"Who allows you?" asked the duck.

"We allow each other," said Mr. Gregg.

"Very nice," said the duck. "And now *we* are going to allow each other to shoot you."

BOOKS FOR CHILDREN BY ROALD DAHL

ROALD DAHL

The Magic Finger

Illustrated by Tony Ross

Puffin Books

PUFFIN BOOKS
Published by the Penguin Group
Penguin Books USA Inc., 375 Hudson Street, New York, New York 10014, U.S.A.
Penguin Books Ltd, 27 Wrights Lane, London W8 5TZ, England
Penguin Books Australia Ltd, Ringwood, Victoria, Australia
Penguin Books Canada Ltd, 10 Alcorn Avenue, Toronto, Ontario, Canada M4V 3B2
Penguin Books (N.Z.) Ltd, 182–190 Wairau Road, Auckland 10, New Zealand

Penguin Books Ltd, Registered Offices: Harmondsworth, Middlesex, England

First published in the United States of America by HarperCollins Children's
Books, a division of HarperCollins Publishers, 1966
First published in Great Britain by Allen & Unwin, 1968
Published in Puffin Books (UK), 1974
Re-issued with new illustrations, 1989
Published in Puffin Books, a division of Penguin Books USA Inc., 1993

10   9   8   7   6   5   4   3   2   1

LIBRARY OF CONGRESS CATALOGING-IN-PUBLICATION DATA
Dahl, Roald.
   The magic finger / by Roald Dahl;
illustrated by Tony Ross.   p.   cm.—(A Young Puffin)
   Summary: Angered by a neighboring family's sport hunting, an eight-
year-old girl turns her magic finger on them.
   ISBN 0-14-036303-3
   [1. Hunting—Fiction.   2. Magic—Fiction.]   I. Ross, Tony, ill.
II. Title.
[PZ7.D1515Mag   1993]   [Fic]—dc20   92-31443

Printed in the United States of America
Set in Palatino

This Book is for Ophelia and Lucy

The farm next to ours is owned by Mr and Mrs Gregg. The Greggs have two children, both of them boys. Their names are Philip and William. Sometimes I go over to their farm to play with them.

I am a girl and I am eight years old.

Philip is also eight years old.

William is three years older. He is ten.

What?

Oh, all right, then.

He is eleven.

Last week, something very funny happened to the Gregg family. I am going to tell you about it as best I can.

Now the one thing that Mr Gregg and his two boys loved to do more than anything else was to go hunting. Every Saturday morning they would take their guns and go off into the woods to look for animals and birds to shoot. Even Philip, who was only eight years old, had a gun of his own.

I can't stand hunting. I just can't *stand* it. It doesn't seem right to me that men and boys should kill animals just for the fun they

get out of it. So I used to try to stop Philip and William from doing it. Every time I went over to their farm I would do my best to talk them out of it, but they only laughed at me.

I even said something about it once to Mr Gregg, but he just walked on past me as if I weren't there.

Then, one Saturday morning, I saw Philip and William coming out of the woods with their father, and they were carrying a lovely young deer.

This made me so cross that I started shout-
ing at them.

The boys laughed and made faces at me,
and Mr Gregg told me to go home and
mind my own P's and Q's.

Well, that did it!

I saw red.

And before I was able to stop myself, I
did something I never meant to do.

I PUT THE MAGIC FINGER ON
THEM ALL!

Oh, dear! Oh, dear! I even put it on Mrs Gregg, who wasn't there. I put it on the whole Gregg family.

For months I had been telling myself that I would never put the Magic Finger upon anyone again — not after what happened to my teacher, old Mrs Winter.

Poor old Mrs Winter.

One day we were in class, and she was teaching us spelling. 'Stand up,' she said to me, 'and spell cat.'

'That's an easy one,' I said. *'K-a-t.'*

'You are a stupid little girl!' Mrs Winter said.

'I am not a stupid little girl!' I cried. 'I am a very nice little girl!'

'Go and stand in the corner,' Mrs Winter said.

Then I got cross, and I saw red, and I put the Magic Finger on Mrs Winter good and strong, and almost at once . . .

Guess what?

Whiskers began growing out of her face! They were long black whiskers, just like the ones you see on a cat, only much bigger. And how fast they grew! Before we had time to think, they were out to her ears!

Of course the whole class started screaming with laughter, and then Mrs Winter said, 'Will you be so kind as to tell me what you find so madly funny, all of you?'

And when she turned around to write something on the blackboard we saw that she had grown a *tail* as well! It was a huge bushy tail!

I cannot begin to tell you what happened after that, but if any of you are wondering whether Mrs Winter is quite all right again now, the answer is No. And she never will be.

The Magic Finger is something I have been able to do all my life.

I can't tell you just *how* I do it, because I

don't even know myself.

But it always happens when I get cross, when I see red . . .

Then I get very, very hot all over . . .

Then the tip of the forefinger of my right hand begins to tingle most terribly . . .

And suddenly a sort of flash comes out of me, a quick flash, like something electric.

It jumps out and touches the person who has made me cross . . .

And after that the Magic Finger is upon him or her, and things begin to happen . . .

Well, the Magic Finger was now upon the whole of the Gregg family, and there was no taking it off again.

I ran home and waited for things to happen.

They happened fast.

I shall now tell you what those things were. I got the whole story from Philip and William the next morning, after it was all over.

In the afternoon of the very same day that I put the Magic Finger on the Gregg family, Mr Gregg and Philip and William went out hunting once again. This time they were going after wild ducks, so they headed towards the lake.

In the first hour they got ten birds.

In the next hour they got another six.

'What a day!' cried Mr Gregg. 'This is the best yet!' He was beside himself with joy.

Just then four more wild ducks flew over their heads. They were flying very low. They were easy to hit.

BANG! BANG! BANG! BANG! went the guns.

The ducks flew on.

'We missed!' said Mr Gregg. 'That's funny.'

Then, to everyone's surprise, the four ducks turned around and came flying right back to the guns.

'Hey!' said Mr Gregg. 'What on earth are they doing? They are really asking for it this time!' He shot at them again. So did the boys. And again they all missed!

Mr Gregg got very red in the face. 'It's the light,' he said. 'It's getting too dark to see. Let's go home.'

So they started for home, carrying with them the sixteen birds they had shot before.

But the four ducks would not leave them alone. They now began flying around and around the hunters as they walked away.

Mr Gregg did not like it one bit. 'Be off!' he cried, and he shot at them many more times, but it was no good. He simply could not hit them. All the way home those four ducks flew around in the sky above their heads, and nothing would make them go away.

Late that night, after Philip and William had gone to bed, Mr Gregg went outside to get some wood for the fire.

He was crossing the yard when all at once he heard the call of a wild duck in the sky.

He stopped and looked up. The night was very still. There was a thin yellow moon over the trees on the hill, and the sky was filled with stars. Then Mr Gregg heard the noise of wings flying low over his head, and he saw the four ducks, dark against the night sky, flying very close together. They were going around and around the house.

Mr Gregg forgot about the firewood, and hurried back indoors. He was now quite afraid. He did not like what was going on. But he said nothing about it to Mrs Gregg. All he said was, 'Come on, let's go to bed. I feel tired.'

So they went to bed and to sleep.

When morning came, Mr Gregg was the first to wake up.

He opened his eyes.

He was about to put out a hand for his watch, to see the time.

But his hand wouldn't come out.

'That's funny,' he said. Where is my hand?'

He lay still, wondering what was up.

Maybe he had hurt that hand in some way?

He tried the other hand.

That wouldn't come out either.

He sat up.

Then, for the first time, he saw what he looked like!

He gave a yell and jumped out of bed.

Mrs Gregg woke up. And when she saw Mr Gregg standing there on the floor, *she* gave a yell, too.

For he was now a tiny little man!

He was maybe as tall as the seat of a chair, but no taller.

And where his arms had been, he had a pair of duck's wings instead!

'But . . . but . . . but . . .' cried Mrs Gregg, going purple in the face. 'My dear man, what's happened to you?'

'What's happened to both of us, you mean!' shouted Mr Gregg.

It was Mrs Gregg's turn now to jump out of bed.

She ran to look at herself in the glass. But she was not tall enough to see into it. She was even smaller than Mr Gregg, and she, too, had got wings instead of arms.

'Oh! Oh! Oh! Oh!' sobbed Mrs Gregg.

'This is witches' work!' cried Mr Gregg. And both of them started running around the room, flapping their wings.

A minute later Philip and William burst in.

The same thing had happened to them. They had wings and no arms. And they were *really* tiny. They were about as big as robins.

'Mama! Mama! Mama!' chirruped Philip. 'Look, Mama, we can fly!' And they flew up into the air.

'Come down at once!' said Mrs Gregg. 'You're much too high!' But before she could say another word, Philip and William had flown right out the window.

Mr and Mrs Gregg ran to the window and looked out. The two tiny boys were now high up in the sky.

Then Mrs Gregg said to Mr Gregg, 'Do you think *we* could do that, my dear?'

'I don't see why not,' Mr Gregg said. 'Come on, let's try.'

Mr Gregg began to flap his wings hard, and all at once, up he went.

Then Mrs Gregg did the same.

'Help!' she cried as she started going up. 'Save me!'

'Come on,' said Mr Gregg. 'Don't be afraid.'

So out the window they flew, far up into the sky, and it did not take them long to catch up with Philip and William.

Soon the whole family was flying around and around together.

'Oh, isn't it lovely!' cried William. 'I've always wanted to know what it feels like to be a bird!'

'Your wings are not getting tired, are they, dear?' Mr Gregg asked Mrs Gregg.

'Not at all,' Mrs Gregg said. 'I could go on for ever!'

'Hey, look down there!' said Philip. 'Somebody is walking in our garden!'

They all looked down, and there below them, in their own garden, they saw four *enormous* wild ducks! The ducks were as big as men, and what is more, they had great long arms, like men, instead of wings.

The ducks were walking in a line to the door of the Greggs' house, swinging their arms and holding their beaks high in the air.

'Stop!' called the tiny Mr Gregg, flying down low over their heads. 'Go away! That's my house!'

The ducks looked up and quacked. The first one put out a hand and opened the door of the house

and went in. The others went in after him.
The door shut.

The Greggs flew down and sat on the
wall near the door. Mrs Gregg began to cry.

'Oh, dear! Oh, dear!' she sobbed. 'They have taken our house. What *shall* we do? We have no place to go!'

Even the boys began to cry a bit now.

'We will be eaten by cats and foxes in the night!' said Philip.

'I want to sleep in my own bed!' said William.

'Now then,' said Mr Gregg. 'It isn't any

good crying. That won't help us. Shall I tell you what we are going to do?'

'What?' they said.

Mr Gregg looked at them and smiled. 'We are going to build a nest.'

'A nest!' they said. 'Can we do that?'

'We *must* do it,' said Mr Gregg. 'We've got to have somewhere to sleep. Follow me.'

They flew off to a tall tree, and right at the top of it Mr Gregg chose the place for the nest.

'Now we want sticks,' he said. 'Lots and lots of little sticks. Off you go, all of you, and find them and bring them back here.'

'But we have no hands!' said Philip.

'Then use your mouths.'

Mrs Gregg and the children flew off. Soon they were back, carrying sticks in their mouths.

Mr Gregg took the sticks and started to build the nest.

'More,' he said. 'I want more and more and more sticks. Keep going.'

The nest began to grow. Mr Gregg was very good at making the sticks stick together.

After a while he said, 'That's enough sticks. Now I want leaves and feathers and things like that to make the inside nice and soft.'

The building of the nest went on and on. It took a long time. But at last it was finished.

'Try it,' said Mr Gregg, hopping back. He was very pleased with his work.

'Oh, isn't it lovely!' cried Mrs Gregg, going into it and sitting down. 'I feel I might lay an egg any moment!'

The others all got in beside her.

'How warm it is!' said William.

'And what fun to be living so high up,' said Philip. 'We may be small, but nobody can hurt us up here.'

'But what about food?' said Mrs Gregg. 'We haven't had a thing to eat all day.'

'That's right,' Mr Gregg said. 'So we will now fly back to the house and go in by an open window and get the tin of biscuits when the ducks aren't looking.'

'Oh, we will be pecked to bits by those dirty great ducks!' cried Mrs Gregg.

'We shall be very careful, my love,' said Mr Gregg. And off they went.

But when they got to the house, they found

all the windows and doors closed. There was no way in.

'Just look at that beastly duck cooking at my stove!' cried Mrs Gregg as she flew past the kitchen window. 'How dare she!'

'And look at *that* one holding my lovely gun!' shouted Mr Gregg.

'One of them is lying in my bed!' yelled
William, looking into a top window.

'And one of them is playing with my electric train!' cried Philip.

'Oh, dear! Oh, dear!' said Mrs Gregg. 'They have taken over our whole house! We shall never get it back. And what *are* we going to eat?'

'I will *not* eat worms,' said Philip. 'I would rather die.'

'Or slugs,' said William.

Mrs Gregg took the two boys under her wings and hugged them. 'Don't worry,' she said. 'I can mince it all up very fine and you won't even know the difference. Lovely slug-burgers. Delicious wormburgers.'

'Oh no!' cried William.

'Never!' said Philip.

'Disgusting!' said Mr Gregg. 'Just because we have wings, we don't have to eat bird food. We shall eat apples instead. Our trees are full of them. Come on!'

So they flew off to an apple tree.

But to eat an apple without holding it in your hands is not at all easy. Every time you try to get your teeth into it, it just pushes away. In the end, they were able to get a few small bites each. And then it began to get dark, so they all flew back to the nest and lay down to sleep.

It must have been at about this time that I, back in my own house, picked up the telephone and tried to call Philip. I wanted to see if the family was all right.

'Hello,' I said.

'Quack!' said a voice at the other end.

'Who is it?' I asked.

'Quack-quack!'

'Philip,' I said, 'is that you?'

'Quack-quack-quack-quack-quack!'

'Oh, stop it!' I said.

Then there came a very funny noise. It was like a bird laughing.

I put down the telephone quickly.

'Oh, that Magic Finger!' I cried. 'What *has* it done to my friends?'

That night, while Mr and Mrs Gregg and
Philip and William were trying to get some
sleep up in the high nest, a great wind began
to blow. The tree rocked from side to side,
and everyone, even Mr Gregg, was afraid
that the nest would fall down. Then came
the rain. It rained and rained, and the water
ran into the nest and they all got as wet as
could be — and oh, it was a bad, bad night!

At last the morning came, and with it the warm sun.

'Well!' said Mrs Gregg. 'Thank goodness that's over! I never want to sleep in a nest again!' She got up and looked over the side . . .

'Help!' she cried. 'Look! Look down there!'

'What is it, my love?' said Mr Gregg. He stood up and peeped over the side.

He got the surprise of his life!

On the ground below them stood the four enormous ducks, as tall as men, and three of them were holding guns in their hands. One had Mr Gregg's gun, one had Philip's gun, and one had William's gun.

The guns were all pointing right up at the nest.

'No! No! No!' called out Mr and Mrs Gregg, both together. 'Don't shoot! Please don't shoot!'

'Why not?' said one of the ducks. It was the one who wasn't holding a gun. 'You are always shooting at *us*.'

'Oh, but that's not the same!' said Mr Gregg. 'We are *allowed* to shoot ducks!'

'Who allows you?' asked the duck.

'We allow each other,' said Mr Gregg.

'Very nice,' said the duck. 'And now *we* are going to allow each other to shoot you.'

(I would have loved to have seen Mr Gregg's face just then.)

'Oh, *please!*' cried Mrs Gregg. 'My two little children are up here with us! You wouldn't shoot my *children!*'

'Yesterday you shot *my* children,' said the duck. 'You shot all six of my children.'

'I'll never do it again!' cried Mr Gregg. 'Never, never, never!'

'Do you really mean that?' asked the duck.

'I *do* mean it!' said Mr Gregg. 'I'll never shoot another duck as long as I live!'

'That is not good enough,' said the duck. 'What about deer?'

'I'll do anything you say if you will only put down those guns!' cried Mr Gregg. 'I'll never shoot another duck or another deer or anything else again!'

'Will you give me your word on that?' said the duck.

'I will! I will!' said Mr Gregg.

'Will you throw away your guns?' asked the duck.

'I will break them into tiny bits!' said Mr Gregg. 'And never again need you be afraid of me or my family.'

'Very well,' said the duck. 'You may now come down.

'And by the way, may I congratulate you on the nest. For a first effort it's pretty good.'

Mr and Mrs Gregg and Philip and William hopped out of the nest and flew down.

Then all at once everything went black before their eyes, and they couldn't see. At the same time a funny feeling came over them all, and they heard a great wind blowing in their ears. Then the black that was before their eyes turned to blue, to green, to red, and then to gold, and suddenly, there they

were, standing in lovely bright sunshine in their own garden, near their own house, and everything was back to normal once again.

'Our wings have gone!' cried Mr Gregg. 'And our arms have come back!'

'And we are not tiny any more!' laughed Mrs Gregg. 'Oh, I am so glad!'

Philip and William began dancing about with joy.

Then, high above their heads, they heard
the call of a wild duck. They all looked up,
and they saw the four birds, lovely against
the blue sky, flying very close together,
heading back to the lake in the woods.

It must have been about half an hour later that I myself walked into the Greggs' garden. I had come to see how things were

going, and I must admit I was expecting the worst. At the gate I stopped and stared. It was a queer sight.

In one corner Mr Gregg was smashing all three guns into tiny pieces with a huge hammer.

In another corner Mrs Gregg was placing beautiful flowers upon sixteen tiny mounds of soil which I learned later were the graves of the ducks that had been shot the day before.

And in the middle of the yard stood Philip
and William, with a sack of their father's best
barley beside them. They were surrounded
by ducks, doves, pigeons, sparrows, robins,
larks, and many other kinds that I did not
know, and the birds were eating the barley
that the boys were scattering by the handful.

'Good morning, Mr Gregg,' I said.

Mr Gregg lowered his hammer and looked
at me. 'My name is not Gregg any more,' he

said. 'In honour of my feathered friends, I have changed it from Gregg to Egg.'

'And I am Mrs Egg,' said Mrs Gregg.

'What happened?' I asked. They seemed to have gone completely dotty, all four of them.

Philip and William then began to tell me the whole story. When they had finished, William said, 'Look! There's the nest! Can

you see it? Right up in the top of the tree! That's where we slept last night!'

'I built it *all* myself,' Mr Egg said proudly. 'Every stick of it.'

'If you don't believe us,' Mrs Egg said, 'just go into the house and take a look at the bathroom. It's a mess.'

'They filled the tub right up to the brim,' Philip said. 'They must have been swimming around in it all night! And feathers everywhere!'

'Ducks like water,' Mr Egg said. 'I'm glad they had a good time.'

Just then, from somewhere over by the lake, there came a loud BANG!

'Someone's shooting!' I cried.

'That'll be Jim Cooper,' Mr Egg said. 'Him and his three boys. They're shooting mad, those Coopers are, the whole family.'

Suddenly I started to see red . . .

Then I got very hot all over . . .

Then the tip of my finger began tingling most terribly. I could feel the power building up and up inside me . . .

I turned and started running towards the lake as fast as I could.

'Hey!' shouted Mr Egg. 'What's up? Where are you going?'

'To find the Coopers,' I called back.

'But why?'

'You wait and see!' I said. 'They'll be nesting in the trees tonight, every one of them!'